For Willa, Elspeth, Myra Jean, Max, and Miles
—Papa Tom

For my son Will
—John

And for all the classroom and music teachers
who pass the music, and this song, along
—Tom and John

To Emerson—I hope you get to see all the wonders
this pretty planet has to offer
—L. W.

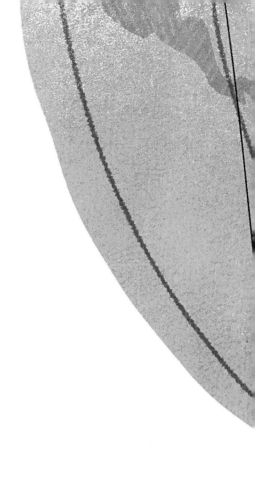

ATHENEUM BOOKS FOR YOUNG READERS

An imprint of Simon & Schuster Children's Publishing Division

1230 Avenue of the Americas, New York, New York 10020

Text copyright © 1988 and 2000 by Limousine Music Co. &
The Last Music Co. (ASCAP)

Illustrations copyright © 2020 by Lee White

Sheet music on endpapers copyright © 1988 and 2000 by
Limousine Music Co. & The Last Music Co. (ASCAP). All Rights Reserved.

All rights reserved, including the right of reproduction in whole or
in part in any form.

ATHENEUM BOOKS FOR YOUNG READERS is a registered
trademark of Simon & Schuster, Inc. Atheneum logo is a trademark
of Simon & Schuster, Inc.

For information about special discounts for bulk purchases, please
contact Simon & Schuster Special Sales at 1-866-506-1949 or
business@simonandschuster.com.

The Simon & Schuster Speakers Bureau can bring authors to your
live event. For more information or to book an event, contact the
Simon & Schuster Speakers Bureau at 1-866-248-3049 or visit our
website at www.simonspeakers.com.

Book design by Debra Sfetsios-Conover

The text for this book was set in Stempel Schneidler Std.

The illustrations for this book were rendered digitally.

Manufactured in China

0820 SCP

First Edition

10 9 8 7 6 5 4 3 2 1

Library of Congress Cataloging-in-Publication Data

Names: Chapin, Tom, author. | Forster, John, 1948– author. | White, Lee,
1970– illustrator.

Title: This pretty planet / by Tom Chapin and John Forster ; illustrated by
Lee White.

Description: First edition. | New York City : Atheneum Books for Young
Readers, [2020] | Audience: Ages 4–8. | Audience: Grades 2–3. | Summary.
Provides lyrics and, on the endpapers, sheet music to a song about the
pretty planet that spins through space, keeping us safe night and day.

Identifiers: LCCN 2019036028 | ISBN 9781534445321 (hardcover) |
ISBN 9781534445338 (eBook)

Subjects: LCSH: Children's songs, English—United States—Texts. | CYAC:
Earth (Planet)—Songs and music. | Songs.

Classification: LCC PZ7.C3654 Thi 2020 | DDC [E]—dc23

LC record available at https://lccn.loc.gov/2019036028

THIS PRETTY PLANET

by Tom Chapin and John Forster
illustrated by Lee White

ATHENEUM BOOKS FOR YOUNG READERS
New York London Toronto Sydney New Delhi

Winds blow. Tides flow.

Shooting stars descend.

Our lives begin,

middle,

and end on . . .

This pretty planet
spinning through space.

You're a garden.
You're a harbor.

You're a holy place.

Golden sun going down.

Gentle blue giant, spin us around.

All through the night,
safe till the morning light.

Time flies.

Ages go by.

PYRAMIDS

MAYFLOWER VOYAGE

Empires rise and fall.

INDUSTRIAL REVOLUTION

SPACE TRAVEL

LAIKA

ROMAN COLOSSEUM

RENAISSANCE

All history led you to me on . . .

INFORMATION AGE

This pretty planet
spinning through space.

You're a garden.

You're a garden.

You're a harbor.

You're a holy place.

Golden sun going down.

Gentle blue giant, spin us around.

All through the night,
safe till the morning light.

THIS PRETTY PLANET

A Three-Part Round for the Round Earth

PHRASE 1

This pret - ty plan - et spin - ning through space. You're a

gar - den. You're a har - bor. You're a ho - ly place.

PHRASE 2

Gold - en sun go - ing down.